P9-CTP-582

PALM BEACH COUNTY
LIBRARY SYSTEM
3650 Summit Boulevard
West Palm Beach, FL 33406-4198

JONATHAN and the BIG BLUE BOAT

Philip C. Stead

A NEAL PORTER BOOK
ROARING BROOK PRESS
NEW YORK

Copyright © 2011 by Philip C. Stead

A Neal Porter Book

Published by Roaring Brook Press

Roaring Brook Press is a division of Holtzbrinck Publishing Holdings Limited Partnership

175 Fifth Avenue, New York, New York 10010

www.roaringbrookpress.com

All rights reserved

Distributed in Canada by H. B. Fenn and Company Ltd.

Library of Congress Cataloging-in-Publication Data

Stead, Philip C.

Jonathan and the big blue boat / Philip C. Stead. — 1st ed.

p. cm.

"A Neal Porter Book."

Summary: When Jonathan's parents decide that he has gotten too old to have a stuffed animal, they trade his favorite bear, Frederick, for a toaster, so he sets off aboard a boat, looking for Frederick.

ISBN: 978-1-59643-562-9

[1. Voyages and travels—Fiction. 2. Boats and boating—Fiction. 3. Teddy bears—Fiction.] I. Title.

PZ7.S808566Jo 2011

[E]—dc22

2010012952

Roaring Brook Press books are available for special promotions and premiums.

For details contact: Director of Special Markets, Holtzbrinck Publishers.

First Edition 2011

Printed in February 2011 in China by South China Printing Co. Ltd., Dongguan City, Guangdong Province

10 9 8 7 6 5 4 3 2 1

To Frederick

"It makes me feel very small," said Jonathan to Frederick. He held Frederick up high so he could see the Big Blue Boat too.

Jonathan loved the Big Blue Boat. He and Frederick would stay at the old wharf till sunset, looking up at its rusty blue hull.

Globe into two
Every circle
the Globe from
also divides its
POSTAGE
1953
PLACE
POSTAL
STAMP
PEB 29 1904

One afternoon Jonathan's parents announced, "You're getting too old for a stuffed animal. So we traded your bear for a toaster." "Oh, no!" cried Jonathan. Frederick was his best friend. "Toasters really are useful," they added.

That day Jonathan walked to the old wharf alone.

13
11

"Ahoy!" called the gray-haired tugboat captain. "Why so sad?"
Jonathan sighed. "Frederick is missing. He could be anywhere in the whole world by now."
The seagulls made a lonely sound over the harbor.
"A long time ago," said the captain, "the Big Blue Boat sailed all over the world. My tugboat worked very hard in those days."
Standing in the shadow of the Big Blue Boat, Jonathan had an idea.

Longitude
West
180
Longitude
Western Continent
Rained all afternoon

Before long the Big Blue Boat was steaming like a tea kettle. The tugboat pulled it out past the buoys and into the open ocean. Jonathan was off to find Frederick.

"Good luck!" the captain bellowed as Jonathan waved goodbye.

And that is how Jonathan came to sail the sea on a Big Blue Boat.

A storm gathered on the high seas. All through the night the Big Blue Boat rocked back and forth on the tall waves.

When morning came the boat was marooned. "Hello," said Jonathan to a mountain goat. "I'm looking for a bear named Frederick."
The goat was startled. He had never met a sea captain before.
"I've never met a bear before," said the goat, "but someday I would like to."
Jonathan looked up. "I could use a first mate," he offered, "but my boat is stuck."
The goat wagged his chin thoughtfully. He wedged his powerful horns beneath the boat's hull. The great ship teetered like a seesaw and then . . .

Below 8 inches.
Between 8 and 24 inches.
Over 80 inches.
Mean Annual Rainfall.
NAUTICAL GUID
RULES OF THE ROAD
MARINE RADIOTELEPHONE PRC
DISTRESS SIGNALS
ASIC RULES OF THE ROAD
HISTLE SIGNALS
—INLAND OR PILOT—
LONG BLAST—
10 to 12 seconds.
SIGNAL
TIC OCEAN

"Anchors aweigh!"

And that is how Jonathan and a mountain goat came to sail the sea on a Big Blue Boat.

Circus tents appeared in the distance.
"Full steam ahead!" said Jonathan to the goat.

Onshore the circus was deserted except for an elephant.
"We're looking for a bear named Frederick," said Jonathan.
"I'm the only one here," the elephant replied. He lowered his trunk. "I've grown too old for the circus." The elephant looked very sad and very wise.
"We could use an experienced traveler," said Jonathan.

PEANUTS
THAILAND
POSTAGE

BURMA POSTAGE
Arabian Sea
Japan Sea
Bombay
Bengal
Black Sea

And that is how Jonathan, a mountain goat, and a circus elephant came to sail the sea on a Big Blue Boat.

"Pirates!" cried the elephant from the lookout perch.
"Arrr! Hand over yer treasure," ordered the pirate captain.
"We're looking for a bear named Frederick," explained Jonathan.
"They're holdin' out on us!" roared the pirate captain. "Ready the arrr-tillery! Storm the ship!"
The goat wielded his horns. The elephant stood on his hind legs, waving his tusks in the air.
"Fire!" the pirate captain yelled.

KER-BLAMMM!!!

Startled by the sound of his own cannon, the captain cried, "Retreat!"

The Big Blue Boat began to sink.
"Oh, no!" cried the goat.
"We're shipwrecked," moaned the elephant.
"Man the lifeboats!" ordered Jonathan.

Just then, a whale swam up from under the fray, balancing the Big Blue Boat on the length of his back. He said, in a deep, slow whale voice, "The ocean can be lonely. It's good to have company."

POST CAR
THIS SIDE IS FOR THE
ONE CENT
TWO
Gulf of Mexico
Cuba
and Circles upon th
E WATER.
Fig. 1.

And that is how Jonathan, a mountain goat, and a circus elephant came to sail the sea on a Big Blue Boat on the back of a whale.

Sun.
Of course every Scholar will be inter
in this Niagara Falls
POST CARD
will be anxious to obtain a full set of this elegant series. This
may be done by having either of your parents or guardians call with you
beautiful
Greylock M
CHICAGO, ILL.
East and West.—East is the direc
West is the direction in which it sets.
II. North and South.—If you stan
toward the west, then
THE EARTH AND ITS
TO BE USED AT THE DISCRETION
Sept 23
the southern
SOLSTICE

The elephant and goat snored like a foghorn and a whistle, "ooooOHaaaah . . . eeeeee . . . oooOHaaaah . . . eeeeee . . ." Jonathan looked out at the endless sea. "Will I ever find Frederick?" he wondered.

Far off a lighthouse blinked, showing the way to a distant port. "Captain?" asked the whale. "Should we set a course?"

THE SOLAR SYSTEM.
The arrow-points show the direction of the motion.
DISTANCES OF THE PLANETS FROM THE SUN.
The Planets are shown about 100 times too large.
Millions of Miles
Jupiter with Satellites
Orbit of the Asteroids
Mercury
Venus
SUN
Earth
Mars
Orbit of Jupiter
PERIODS OF REVOLUTION and mean Distances of the Pla
Mercury 88 Days 36 Mil. M. Jupiter
Planets upon their Axes.
Moon, 27d. 7h. 43m.
Venus, 0d. 23h. 50 m.?
Mars, 1d. 0h. 37m.
Saturn, 0d. 10h. 14.4m.
Neptune, Unknown
LATITUDE 40°.
THE PLANETS.
Scale, 1 : 3,000,000,000.
URANUS
NEPTUNE
SATURN
MOON
Emerging from the Shadows
Earth Shadow
Ship Argo
Southern Cross
Centaurus
Scorpio
Libra
Hercules
Sextans
Ophiuchus
Wolf (Lupus)
Altar
Norma
Musca
Pole
Polaris
Rasalhague
Kochab
Pherkad
Vega
Deneb
Denebola
Regulus
Antares
Equator
Zodiac
Orbit of Jupiter

"I'll watch the ship," said the whale.
The others spent the day bear hunting in train stations and alleyways.
They rode taxicabs and elevators and talked to pigeons along the way. Frederick was nowhere to be found.
"Where will we look now?" asked the elephant.
A light flickered on in a shop window.
"We'll try here," said Jonathan.

SHOP
5 CENTS 5
POSTAGE
UNITED STATES OF AMERICA
25c
POSTES
15c
REPUBLIQUE FR
UNITED STATES POSTAGE
12 CENTS 12
SCHOOL NUMBER 7
BALTIMORE PUBLIC SCHOOLS
SCHOOL NUMBER 7
BALTIMORE PUBLIC SCHOOLS
ON'S READING CHARTS.—A series of twenty-four
and printed in type that may be read in any part of th
ON'S PRIMER.—Just published. 60 pages.
ON'S FIRST READER. " 80 pages.
ON'S SECOND READER. " 192 pages.
ON'S THIRD READER. " 224 pages.
ON'S FOURTH READER.
ON'S FIFTH READER.
books may be used independently of the char's.
ding feature, common to the charts and books,
on, consists in the arrangement by which teachers may proceed by the word method
thod, or alphabet method, with equal facility, according to their preferences.
ter's Natural Series of Arithmetics.
'S PRIMARY ARITHMETIC.—Fully illustrated
pages. With answers.
NEON GLOW LAMP
MADE IN U.S.A.
GENERAL ELECTRIC
VAPOR LAMP COMPANY
Hoboken, N.J.
PATENTS
1,498,908
1,951,
ALSO ONE OR MORE
OF THE FOLLOWING
1,481,
1,374,679
1,652,826
1,965,5
1,964,589
NEON GLOW LAMP
MADE IN U.S.A.

Inside, the shop was cluttered but cheerful.

"Hello," said a little girl from behind the counter. In her arms she was holding . . .

"FREDERICK!" cried Jonathan.

"Oh, he's not for sale," said the little girl. "I traded a toaster for this bear. He is my best friend. I wouldn't go anywhere without him."

Jonathan smiled. After all, a big boat needs a big crew.

S
Z
D
25
$
NATIONAL BANK OF BA
BAY CITY, MICHIGAN
Paid for
Apr 19

And that is how Jonathan, Frederick, a mountain goat, a circus elephant, and the little girl from behind the counter came to sail the sea on a Big Blue Boat on the back of a whale.